For Abi and Darren

Published by Jenny Witchard
Text and illustrations copyright ©Jenny Witchard 2022
The right of Jenny Witchard to be identified as the author and illustrator
of this work has been asserted by her in accordance with the
Copyright Designs and Patents Act 1988

This is my grandson, Stanley, who has a sister called Isla and a cousin whose name is Martha.

When Stanley was little and came to my house for sleepovers, I used to make up stories for him about a boy called Stanley who did very ordinary things, but whenever he shouted, "Look at me," strange, magical things happened and he had some adventures.

On those adventures Stanley became Stan the Man.

Jenny Witchard

Stan the Man

and the
Flying Bed

by Jenny Witchard

Stanley was happy.
Today was the day
He was going to Grandpa
And Grandma's to stay.

He put on his new specs
And dressed really fast...

Then packed up his bag and was ready at last.

Then off Stanley sped in Dad's big red car.
So it didn't take long as it wasn't too far.
Dad turned a corner, then drove really slow

And stopped right outside Grandma's bungalow.

Dad had to leave,
So waved Stanley goodbye,
Who felt a bit sad
And a little bit shy.

But Grandpa and Grandma
Were there by the door.
So he gave them a hug,
Threw his stuff
On the floor....

Then ran down the hall and had a quick peep
At the little room where
Stanley knew he would sleep.

But Stanley could hardly
Believe his own eyes...

Grandpa had built him
A MASSIVE surprise!!!

Where Stanley normally
Found his old bed,

A fantastic aeroplane
Stood there instead.
It was actually a bed
That was up in the air
But it looked like a plane
With a short wooden stair.

He climbed up the steps, and sat on his bed.
He liked the old one but preferred this instead.
Stanley then knelt and pretended to fly.
He spread out his arms and then gave his cry....

You've guessed it!
Those magical things
All began!

His feet began tingling,
Some lights swirled about.
The bed started shaking.
Stan thought he'd fall out!

Just then from the bed
Came a loud roaring sound
And the whirr of propellers
That went round and round.
Stan started shrinking
And so did the bed!
Then Stan the Man found
A strange hat on his head!

Stan and the bed

Had become very small

And the bed was no longer

For sleeping at all!

The aeroplane bed

Had become a real plane.

A very small one,

But a plane just the same.

Then with a roar
The plane started to fly.
It flew round the room,
Not up in the sky.

"This is great fun,"
Stan thought, "I want more."
The plane thought the same
And flew out of the door!

It flew down the hall
And Stan was then shown
That the mischievous plane
Had a mind of its own!

'Cause off the plane dashed
With a big burst of power...
Swept into the bathroom
And whizzed past the shower.

The plane missed the taps
And the towel rail too
But Stanley was scared
They'd crash into the loo!

It entered the lounge,
Then zoomed round the light,
And gave Stan's poor Grandma
A terrible fright!

Grandpa then ducked as they flew overhead.
He looked very worried, but then Grandpa said,

"Now listen young Stanley,
Just grab the controls.
Take over the flying
Before that plane rolls."

Stan listened to Grandpa –
Did what he was told.
He gave good advice
(Though he was quite old.)
Now Stan could order
The plane where to go.
He could make it go fast
Or go very slow.

Then feeling excited, Stan guided the plane
Out through a window and off down the lane.

He crossed a big park, and flew over a school.
But what he saw next Stan thought very cool.

Far down below him,
Stan saw the sea.

"I like this adventure,"
He thought happily.

A seagull was startled
As Stan hurtled by
And he just missed a kite
Flying high in the sky.

He soared in the air...
Did a great loop the loop.
But Stan got quite scared
And thought he might poop!

So he levelled the plane and looked all around.

Stan stared at the sky
And gazed at the ground.

Stan then looked up at a noise he had heard
And nearly flew into a strange looking bird!
The bird, which was purple, gave a loud

And to Stan's huge surprise, the bird started to talk!

"I wish that you'd look
Where you're going, young man.
You seem a bit lost.
Do you have a plan?

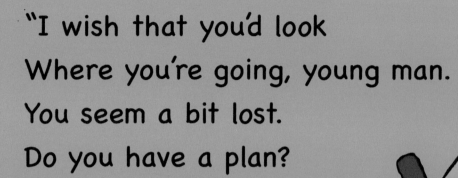

Do you know where you are,
Or you're going to?
Whatever the problem
I'd like to help you."

The strange purple bird asked Stan the Man where His Grandma lived. Then said, "I'll take you straight there."

So Stanley flew off behind 'Strork', the big bird. Not really his name, but it was a word....

That suited Stan's friend and so that was that.
(And Strork liked it too as a matter of fact!)

They both left the sea to fly over the land.

Stan waved to the pier
That looked very grand.

They followed the river
And went past the school,
And then Stan could see
A big swimming pool.
They glided straight on
To fly over the park
And Stan was quite glad
As it soon would be dark.

Then all of a sudden, right down below,
Stan saw his Grandparents' bungalow.
"That's where we're going," he shouted quite loud,
Then followed the bird straight down through a cloud.

Then into the garden... but Stan didn't see
A branch sticking out and a wing hit the tree!
Stan shouted out, "I'm going to crash!"
And the very next second, there was a huge...

The garden pond seemed a good place to land,
As Stan wasn't hurt. On the other hand....
His clothes were all wet and he ached just a bit.
He was glad it was water, not ground he had hit!

Stan swam to the edge
Of the pond and climbed out.
He'd had enough now
So he gave a loud shout....

Look at me,
Look at me,
My name's
Stan the
Man.

Then what happened next?
Have a guess if you can...

Stan began growing. No longer as small
As he'd been in the plane, he now felt quite tall!

No sign of the hat, just hair on his head.
And there Stanley sat on his special 'plane bed.'

Just then, Stanley's Grandpa and Grandma appeared.
"Oh dear," Stanley said, "I just disappeared!"
He then climbed down from the bed in a hurry.
"I'm sorry, I didn't intend you to worry!"

"What do you mean?" Grandma asked with a smile.
"We know you've been playing in here for a while.
But we didn't worry, we knew you were here.
We're certain you never would just disappear!"

So Stanley went out to the garden to play.
It was then that he heard a strorky voice say,
"I'm so glad you're safe. Now I don't want to boast,
But I got you home safely – so where is my toast?"

Stanley gave Strork all the toast he could eat,
And gave him a dollop of jam as a treat.
"I love an adventure" said Stan, "...Now and then.
But I really don't think I'll go flying again."

Have you read the other Stan the Man stories?

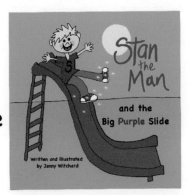

Stan the Man and the Big Purple Slide

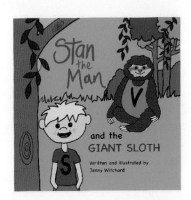

Stan the Man and the Giant Sloth

Stan the Man and the Christmas Adventure

Printed in Great Britain
by Amazon